6/11

Merci Mister Dash!

Monica Kulling

Illustrated by

Esperança Melo

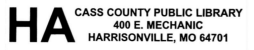
Tundra Books

Published in Canada by Tundra Books,
75 Sherbourne Street, Toronto, Ontario M5A 2P9

Published in the United States by Tundra Books of Northern New York,
P.O. Box 1030, Plattsburgh, New York 12901

Library of Congress Control Number: 2010926096

Library and Archives Canada Cataloguing in Publication

Kulling, Monica, 1952-
    Merci Mister Dash! / Monica Kulling, author ; Esperança Melo,
illustrator.

For children ages 3-6 years.
ISBN 978-0-88776-964-1

    1. Dogs – Juvenile fiction. 2. Picture books for
children. I. Melo, Esperança II. Title.

PS8571.U54M47 2011   jC813'.54   C2010-902060-X

We acknowledge the financial support of the Government of Canada through the Book Publishing Industry Development Program (BPIDP) and that of the Government of Ontario through the Ontario Media Development Corporation's Ontario Book Initiative. We further acknowledge the support of the Canada Council for the Arts and the Ontario Arts Council for our publishing program.

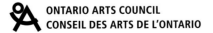

ONTARIO ARTS COUNCIL
CONSEIL DES ARTS DE L'ONTARIO

Medium: acrylic on paper

Design: Leah Springate

Printed and bound in China

1 2 3 4 5 6   16 15 14 13 12 11

*For Nancy and Dr. Cheryl, who encouraged me
to write from my life.
For my mother, who loved French.
For my sister Erica, who flew down the hill.*
M.K.

*For Bill, whose support and enthusiasm inspires
me to new horizons.*
E.M.

I would like to thank Nancy Ennis, Susan Hughes,
and Tara Walker for reading earlier versions of this
story and for their helpful comments. I would also like
to thank Sue Tate for an excellent edit.

Mister Dash was unlike any hound in town. His nose was like a pointer's and his legs were like a Lab's. He had the body of a boxer, a poodle's tail, and a sheepdog's ears. He might look like five different dogs, but Mister Dash was a model of manners. He never jumped on people, or growled, or drooled, or made a mess. He always put his best paw forward.

Mister Dash was also a dapper dresser. He wore a vest and bow tie at breakfast. On his morning jog, he wore a fleece hoodie. In the bright sun, he wore a hat and "doggles." And in winter, Mister Dash braved the snow in cozy boots.

Mister Dash lived with Madame Croissant, who owned a gift shop called *Vive la France!* He loved to help in the shop and greet all the customers with a friendly *woof*. When they bought something, he thanked them with a *woof, woof*.

"Your dog has the best manners," customers would say.

"*Merci!* Mister Dash is most unique," agreed Madame Croissant.

When the day was over, Mister Dash would snooze by her chair while Madame Croissant worked on her stamp collection. She was an avid armchair traveler, with stamps from around the world. Snoozing and stamp collecting made life calm. But Sundays were another story.

On Sundays, Madame Croissant's granddaughter came to visit. Daphne was a wild child. She ran through the house like a racehorse. She pounded down the stairs like a baboon. She hung from the trees like a bat and splashed in the puddles like an elephant. Madame Croissant called her "my little dynamo."

Mister Dash didn't like Madame Croissant's little dynamo. She was loud and rambunctious. She broke things and spilled things and turned life into a whirl-wind. Whenever he saw Daphne coming up the walk, Mister Dash would rush to the park, where he could read the papers in peace.

One Sunday, Mister Dash was all ready for his
morning jog when Daphne roared into the house.
Oh, no! he thought.

"*Bonjour, Grandmère!*" she shouted, slamming
the front door.

"*Bonjour, ma chérie,*" sang Madame Croissant.

"Goody! Mister Dash is here!" yelled Daphne.
"We'll play zoo. I'll be the zookeeper. Mister Dash
will be the wild animal." She grabbed him in a
fierce hug.

Arrrgh! he choked. *There's one wild animal in
this house and it's not me.*

"Gentle, my little cabbage," said Madame
Croissant. "Mister Dash is not a toy."

"I know, *Grandmère!*" shouted Daphne, dancing
on her tiptoes.

What rotten luck, thought Mister Dash. *If I
hadn't stopped to dress, I could be reading in the
park right now.*

"Snack time, then playtime," said Madame
Croissant. "Who would like my world-famous
caramel corn?"

"Pop! Pop! Popcorn!" sang Daphne, hopping
with glee.

There were only a few kernels on Mister Dash's plate. He chewed one at a time, savoring the sweetness. *Crunch. Crunch*.

Daphne didn't savor anything. She crammed fistfuls into her mouth. Caramel corn flew every which-a-way, like snowflakes in a blizzard. A piece even landed on Mister Dash's head!

What an indignity, he thought, feeling miserable.

"Playtime!" shouted Daphne, pulling Mister Dash outside.

Madame Croissant joined them in the garden. It was time to prune her roses.

Daphne ran to Mister Dash's deluxe doghouse and started tossing everything out. "Your house will be the zoo cage!" she shouted.

Mister Dash's sheepskin rug sailed over his head. His bone-shaped squeaky toy landed in the roses. Out flew a rubber ball, two bowls, a woolly blanket, his stuffed-toy cat, and a picture of Madame Croissant.

Bonk! The picture hit Mister Dash on the head. *Ouch!*

That was it. *Fini!* He had to get Daphne out of his house. He grabbed her by her pants pocket and pulled. *Rriiipp!* Mister Dash tumbled backward into the dirt. *Ooof!* The pocket hung from his mouth.

"Hey!" yelled Daphne. "Look what you did. I'm telling!"

But Madame Croissant was lost in the luscious world of *les fleurs.*

Mister Dash was dirty from head to paw. Quick as a cricket, Daphne picked up the hose and sprayed him with cold water.

"Messy Mister Dash needs a bath," she giggled.

Mister Dash was soaking wet. He wanted to dry in the sun, but Daphne threw his woolly blanket over his head and started drying him off herself. Fiercely.

"What a cute baby," said Daphne, wrapping Mister Dash in the blanket. Only his eyes peeped through, and they looked angry.

"*Très* cute, my little cabbage," said Madame Croissant, without looking up.

Daphne coaxed her "baby" into her red *Radio Flyer* wagon and walked him down the block. Madame Croissant watched out of the corner of her eye while tending her front-yard flowers.

At the end of the block, Mister Dash jumped out of the wagon and shook himself free of the blanket. *Fini!*

Then Daphne had another idea.

"I'm going flying!" she shouted.

Daphne got into the wagon and shoved off down the hill. She started slowly, but in no time the wagon was tearing down the sidewalk!

"Help! I can't stop!" Daphne cried out.

Mister Dash was halfway home when he heard the screams. *What's this? Is Daphne in trouble?*

Mister Dash left his manners at the top of the hill. He put his Lab legs to good use and ran like a greyhound.

At the bottom of the hill was a large crack.

Racing hard, Mister Dash drew close. When he was close enough, he grabbed Daphne's overall straps and yanked her out of the wagon. Together they rolled down the grassy slope on the other side of the sidewalk.

Mister Dash made sure that Daphne had a soft landing.

"*Merci* Mister Dash!" said Daphne. "You are so brave." She gave him a gentle hug.

Madame Croissant came running.

"My little cabbage is safe," she said. "And Mister Dash is a hero!"

That evening, the house was quiet. Mister Dash
snoozed by the chair while Madame Croissant
studied her stamps through a magnifying glass.
Tomorrow promised to be a perfect day: *There
would be no Daphne!* Mister Dash smiled in his
sleep.